LITTLE
LiON
RESCUE

tiger tales

5 River Road, Suite 128, Wilton, CT 06897
Published in the United States 2020
Originally published in Great Britain 2019
by the Little Tiger Group
Text copyright © 2019 Rachel Delahaye
Inside illustrations copyright © 2019 Jo Anne Davies at Artful Doodlers
Cover illustration copyright © 2019 Suzie Mason
ISBN-13: 978-1-68010-462-2
ISBN-10: 1-68010-462-4
Printed in the USA
STP/4800/0335/0720

For more insight and activities, visit us at www.tigertalesbooks.com

LITTLE
LiON
RESCUE

by Rachel Delahaye

tiger tales

This is dedicated to my grandmother, Rosemary, who
loved animals and fought for their rights
—Rachel

CONTENTS

The Big Clean-Up

"Oh, yuck! You're covered in elephant dung!" Emma held her nose and pointed at Callie's overalls.

"You can't muck out elephants without getting a little bit dirty." Callie grinned. "If you're clean, it means you didn't work hard enough!"

"I'd rather be lazy than stinky," Emma said, flicking mud and straw from her fingers.

Mr. Tom, the zookeeper, clapped his

hands together loudly.

"Shovels down, everyone," he called. "Gather around."

The girls joined the rest of their school group at the gate, where Mr. Tom laughed when he saw them.

"So how was that? Smelly?"

Everyone made gagging noises and giggled.

"Elephants eat for up to sixteen hours a day, which means they produce a lot of … muck. If you look behind you, you'll see the elephants waiting to come back into the enclosure."

The giant gray beasts were behind the next gate, their ears flapping gently.

"I hope they say thank you to us for cleaning their house!" Emma said.

"I think they'll be very glad," Mr. Tom said. "Can you see how their tails are swishing from side to side? It means they're happy."

"How do we know when they're *not* happy?" Callie asked. She wished she had brought a book to take notes.

"I've been lucky enough to spend time with these animals in the wild," Mr. Tom said. "I've seen them in all kinds of moods. If their tails get stiff or they spread their ears out wide, then they may be nervous. If they make a trumpeting sound, then get out of there fast! It could mean they're about to charge."

Callie closed her eyes and imagined it—a happy herd of elephants suddenly startled, ears wide and trunks raised, trumpeting their alarm…. Mr. Tom clapped his hands again and she opened her eyes, hoping no one had seen her daydreaming.

"Okay, these beauties need to come in and cool off in the water. You all could do with some cooling off, too! Your teacher says there's ice cream waiting for you inside, just as soon as you get out of those overalls. Off to the bathrooms!"

There was a big cheer as the children hurried out of the enclosure, shouting "Ice cream, ice cream!" Callie was the last to go. She would stay forever if she could, even if it *was* smelly.

She tugged on the zookeeper's sleeve. "My name is Callie. Can I ask you something?"

"Of course." Over her head, he beckoned to the other zookeepers, who began to lead the herd back into the enclosure. Callie watched them in wonder—how did these large animals move so gracefully?

"Callie, did you have a question?"

"Yes. I'm sorry!" Callie blushed. "I just wanted to know how you became a zookeeper."

"Well, I knew what I wanted to do from a very young age. I learned all I could about animals, and when I was old enough, I volunteered at rescue centers all over Africa. It took a lot of patience and passion, but now I'm here, in charge of elephants and lions. It's my ideal job."

"You're so lucky being with animals all day long."

"Is this what you want to do when you grow up?"

"I want to be a vet," Callie said. "I want to help animals who are in trouble."

"Being a vet is a tough job!" Mr. Tom said. "But it looks to me like you have

determination.
That's a great
start."

"Mr. Tom?"
Callie said,
thinking of
something. "If
you're in charge of the lions, does that
mean you can tell them to wake up?"
She had been so excited for the zoo
trip but with a particular longing to see
those proud creatures up close. The
empty enclosure had left her feeling
disappointed.

Mr. Tom laughed. "It's not that
simple, I'm afraid. I'm sorry your
group didn't get to see them, but if
they wake up before you go, I'll come
and get you, okay?"

In the distance, Callie could hear her friends calling. She wasn't interested in ice cream. She just wanted to talk to Mr. Tom about animals.

"You'd better go," Mr. Tom said, steering her toward the gate. "The elephants are coming, and you're not a professional animal handler—not yet, anyway."

After changing out of her overalls, Callie found Emma in the zoo cafeteria, covered in pink-and-white gunk.

"So, you don't mind getting dirty *sometimes*," Callie said.

"No!" Emma licked the sticky liquid dripping down her wrist. "I don't mind getting messy when it's ice cream. Are you going to have one?"

"I'm too excited to eat!" Callie unfolded her map of the zoo and pointed to an area called Pride of Place—the lion enclosure. "The zookeeper said he'd come and get us as soon as they wake up. Isn't that great?"

"*If* they wake up, Callie. Come on, it's the butterfly house next."

"You'd better wash your hands, then. Butterflies *love* sugar! They'll lick you all over with their long, curly tongues."

Emma shrieked and ran to the bathroom, and Callie smiled.

The butterfly house was going to be fun! But as they walked through the rubber doors and into the steamy room full of colorful fluttering wings,

Callie hoped that Mr. Tom would soon interrupt with the news that the lions had woken up.

Free to Roam

"Ugh, it was so sticky and hot in there," Emma gasped, flapping her hands in front of her face.

"It's because the exotic butterflies need a tropical temperature," said Callie. "I loved the big blue ones, didn't you?"

"No! All I could think about were those tongues!" Emma wrinkled her nose. "I watched one drinking…. Callie, the tongue actually *rolled* out! Butterflies are monsters!"

The teachers did a head count of all the children, most of whom were looking soggy after their butterfly encounter. Mr. Vincent was looking particularly frazzled, but it wasn't because of the butterfly house. Apparently, David, Dan, and Sarah had crept off to get another look at the crocodiles without permission and were now completely lost!

"Mrs. Mullins and I are going to look for some lost students. The rest of you may take one last walk around the zoo," Mr. Vincent said, dabbing at his face with a handkerchief. "Stay in pairs, and meet back at the gift shop in fifteen minutes."

"Anyone who is late will sit in the front of the bus on the way back, next to me," Mrs. Mullins added sternly.

Before she'd even finished speaking, Callie had grabbed Emma's hand and was pulling her along the walkway.

"Whoa, there, Callie! What's the rush?"

"We only have fifteen minutes, and there's so much to see! Come on, this way."

"You're dragging me to the lions, aren't you?" Emma said, jogging to keep up. "I bet that's where we're going."

"Yup!" Callie grinned. "I've got a feeling I'm going to meet one today."

All around them, the zoo rang with the cheeps and hoots of birds and animals, but Pride of Place was disappointingly quiet. Callie read everything on the information boards—about the Serengeti, the lions' native home, and about diet and behavior and bringing up cubs. Then she paced around the enclosure fence, hoping to see one hiding in the bushes or sleeping up on a rock.

"They're not here," Emma said impatiently. "If we wait any longer, there won't be time to see anything else."

It was true. The zoo had more animal species than Callie could name. She wasn't even sure *why* she was so desperate to see the lions. There would be other visits to the zoo.

14

"Emma, you're right," Callie said. "Where should we go next?"

"Let's go-go to the flamingos!" Emma sang. "This way."

It was impossible to be sad when Emma was around, and Callie joined in with her friend's made-up song. They sang *Everybody sing-o, we're going to the flamingos!* at the tops of their voices, and the other visitors looked at them as if they were crazy, which only made Emma sing louder.

At the flamingo pond, Emma tried to stand on one leg for as long as possible while Callie read out facts from the information board.

"Did you know that the feathers under flamingos' wings are black and can only be seen when they are flying? And their pink feathers are only pink because they eat pink shrimp!"

"I thought it was for camouflage," Emma pondered.

"Only if they were hiding in a strawberry field," Callie snorted. "And I don't think there are many of those in Africa!"

Laughing, the girls ran back to the gift shop, discussing what color flamingos would be if they ate blueberries or chocolate or multicolored lollipops.

At the gift shop David, Dan, and Sarah were standing behind Mrs. Mullins, looking sheepish. Mr. Vincent had gone to freshen up—which meant he was having a cup of tea to calm his nerves—so the children were allowed a few minutes to look around the shop and spend their money.

"The gift shop—my favorite enclosure!" Emma cheered.

Callie smiled, but for her, this was the worst part of the zoo. It meant her time with the real animals had come to an end.

"Come on. First to find a fluffy flamingo gets a … a fluffy flamingo, I guess!" Emma whooped and disappeared into the cuddly toy section, along with most of the class. Within seconds, they were all play-acting with squishy crocodiles, plush sharks, and stretchy octopuses.

Callie wasn't really interested in gift-shop toys. For starters, they didn't look that realistic. The sharks' teeth were made of bendy felt, the snakes were *furry*, and the cuddly flamingos did *not* have black feathers under their wings....

Instead, she was drawn to the
postcards, which were photographs of
real animals. She wanted to find one of
a butterfly drinking nectar for Emma.

Just the thought of it made her giggle.
If she saw a penguin, she'd get that for
her mom—it was her favorite animal—
and an elephant for her dad.

But what about a souvenir for
herself? It was so hard to choose. From
the anaconda snake that made her
classmates scream to the foxy-faced
zorro, Callie loved all the animals from
A to Z. She couldn't pick a favorite
if she tried! Maybe a postcard of
the one animal she'd missed on the
day's outing would be a good choice.
It wouldn't be a souvenir, more of
a missing piece. Yes, she would buy
herself a postcard of the lions.

A Particular Postcard

There weren't many lion postcards—a couple taken in the zoo and a few taken in the wild. The ones in the wild didn't show lions as "kings of the jungle" like picture books did, but as kings of the African plains, which were wide, open grasslands that seemed to go on forever. Callie was about to pick one when some other cards farther along the wall caught her eye. They were large, shiny, and colorful.

When she got close, she saw they were

3-D hologram pictures making the animals look like they were alive, and the pictures moved around or changed completely if you tilted them. There were great white sharks swimming then attacking, grizzly bears sitting and then standing tall, and lions, too! There was only one left and Callie grabbed it quickly, as if it might disappear.

She looked down at the picture and gasped at how lifelike it was—it was as if she were holding the lions in the very palm of her hand!

The pride was sitting in the shade of a tree, and all of them were snoozing in the midday sun. All but one. A lioness was standing up, her head turned to the side. It was as if she was looking for something. Callie tilted the card backward. The picture of the pride faded away, and in its place was a single lion cub, standing all alone, its eyes wide with fear. Something was wrong. This lion cub was lost.

Callie bought the card right away. There was no way she could leave this little cub behind, even if it *was* just a picture! She'd give it a home on her bedroom wall, and on the bus ride back, she could pass the time making up a story with a happy ending for the lost cub. Maybe Emma could help with a song. At that very moment, Emma came up behind her, placed a long, cuddly snake on her shoulder, and hissed. Callie jumped back in surprise, but when she saw what it was, she grabbed the snake and cuddled it under her chin.

"You're supposed to be scared!" Emma groaned.

"Not me.... I'd love to meet a real-life snake. I'd like to wear one around my neck like a scarf."

"People would call you Callie with the Cobra Boa!" Emma laughed.

Just then, Mrs. Mullins boomed her full name—Catalina—across the gift shop. Callie looked over and knew that her day was about to get better, because standing beside Mrs. Mullins was Mr. Tom. The lions were finally awake!

Mrs. Mullins announced that she would hold the bus for anyone who wanted to see the lions, but Callie's classmates were more interested in choosing toys and candy for the trip home. Even Emma wasn't that interested. She had bought the cuddly snake and was happily annoying people with it.

"I'm sorry, but we can't delay the ride home for just one student," Mrs. Mullins said. Callie looked at Emma pleadingly and got down on one knee, clasping her hands together.

"Only if you promise to play pranks with me on the way home," Emma said, holding out her second purchase—a

tube of plastic
spiders. Callie
leaped up and
wrapped her
arms around her.

"And I can
promise to have them
back in ten minutes…," Mr. Tom added
with a smile.

Mrs. Mullins caved, and the girls ran
ahead of Mr. Tom, laughing and waving
at the monkeys on the way. When Pride
of Place came into view, Callie sprinted
and didn't stop until she was right there,
her face against the enclosure fence.

"Where are they? Where are they?"
she cried.

Mr. Tom put his hands on his hips
and sighed heavily. "Boab, the big

male lion, was out…. But it seems he's hidden himself away again. Lions are crepuscular, which means they mainly come out at twilight and sleep through the day. Don't take it personally. Visitors are often disappointed. We have webcams dotted around the enclosure, so when you get home, you might be able to see them online."

"Oh, okay," Callie said weakly.

"Come on, Callie," Emma said. "Race you back to the gift shop. Let's tell the others we saw nine huge lions and a million lion cubs and make them jealous."

"But that would be a lie," Callie said sadly.

She took her postcard from her pocket and looked at the pride, imagining them there in front of her. Then she tilted it so she could see the cub.

"Callie!" Emma's voice was impatient, but it sounded oddly quiet, as if she was a long way away. She must have already started running back. It was time to go.

Callie raised her eyes to look at the enclosure one last time, but from out of nowhere, a warm cloud of dust hit her in the face. She blinked and rubbed her eyes.... Even before she opened them again, she knew something strange had happened. The air felt warmer, her skin tingled as if she was standing in strong sunlight, and the echoing zoo sounds were gone.

She opened her eyes and gasped. It couldn't be possible! She had to be dreaming!

In front of her, stretching to the

horizon, was an expanse of dry grasses, bleached white and yellow by the sun. The landscape was bare except for a few lonely trees and occasional lumps of rock, some as big as houses. The sky was a wide roof of the palest blue.

Callie spun around. There was no Emma or Mr. Tom behind her, no information board or fence, no walkway back to the gift shop. This wasn't a trick of the light or a special effect designed by the zoo for a Serengeti experience....

This *was* the Serengeti!

Welcome to the Wild

Callie knew all about the Serengeti National Park in Tanzania. But what she didn't know is how she got there! Was Pride of Place a portal to another dimension? Was Mr. Tom some kind of time-traveling zookeeper? Or maybe.... Callie looked down at the postcard in her hands.

"Did you bring me here?" she asked it. "And how do I get back?"

She tipped the picture backward and

forward to see if it would transport her back to the zoo, but nothing happened. Callie felt a flutter of panic rising in her tummy. If she didn't get back soon, Mrs. Mullins would be angry, and Mr. Vincent would need another cup of tea, and the bus driver might lose her patience and drive off without them all! Then something caught her eye.

In front of her was a rock, and behind it she was sure she saw something move. Callie froze. *Don't be scared*, she told herself. *If it was a big animal, I'd see its horns or ears sticking out above the rock*. She decided it had to be something small, like a bird or a hare, and crept forward to take a look.

At the same time, the creature cautiously peeked around the rock. It wasn't a hare or a bird.

Callie knew exactly what it was.

She held her breath as it walked unsteadily out into the open on large, padded paws.

"Hey, little lion," she said softly.

And it was *definitely* a lion. Callie quickly recognized the roundness of the ears, and even though its little legs had spotty markings like a leopard, she could see the strong, lion-like features through  the fluffy golden coat that covered the rest of its body. There were gray flecks

31

on its wide nose, which was dotted with rows of white whiskers.

Callie crouched down so she wouldn't look tall and scary and held out her hand. The cub was shaking, and its eyes were big and worried. Callie had seen that expression before. She took the postcard from her pocket, tilted it back, and studied it again…. A cub looking lost. She stared back at the real-life cub in front of her.

"It's *you*, isn't it?" she whispered.

The cub made a noise that sounded more like a mouse's squeak than a lion's roar. Callie didn't know whether to laugh or cry at this little creature trying to make its voice heard.

"I can't hear you very well," she said. "How about if I come a little closer?"

She crawled slowly on her hands and knees toward the cub. Frightened, it took a step back.

"I won't hurt you," Callie said, sitting back on her heels. "I'm here to help. I want to be a vet when I grow up, which means I care a lot about animals. You probably don't understand a word I'm saying. You've probably never heard a human talk. Maybe you've never seen a human at all! Well, now you have, and I promise you I'm very friendly."

Callie laughed at herself, talking such gibberish, and imagined what Emma would make of it. She'd say: "You're like Doctor Dolittle, Callie!" But although Callie really did wish she could talk to animals (and *Doctor Dolittle* was her favorite story), what she said didn't need to make sense; it just needed to make the cub feel safe. And it looked as if it was working.

The cub began to take little steps forward, its eyes fixed on her.

"That's it." Callie reached her hand out farther for the cub to sniff. "It's all going to be okay."

The cub rubbed its cheek against the back of her hand, and Callie was able to stretch out her fingers and scratch the

fur behind the
cub's ear. It
closed its eyes
in bliss. When
she stopped, it
shook its head
from side to side

and leaped right up onto her lap.

"Does this mean we're friends?" Callie
laughed, rubbing the cub's back. "Then
we'd better get to know more about each
other. I'm Callie. If you have a name, I
don't think I could pronounce it. I don't
speak lion-ese. I'm ten years old. How
old are you, I wonder?"

The cub wobbled in her lap and fell
off. It bounced back up again.

"Let's take a good look at you," Callie
said, confident that the cub trusted her.

"You're a little bit scrawny, bigger than the average cat, but smaller than a dog. And look at those beautiful wide paws! Hmmm, I'm guessing you're about three months old."

Callie thought back to the information boards at the zoo. It said cubs didn't become independent until they were two years old.

"Alone and so young! You probably still need your mother's milk as well as fresh meat. Oh my goodness, your mother must be worried sick. How on earth did you get lost in the first place?"

Lifting the cub up into her arms, Callie stood and looked around her. She could see herds of gray animals in the distance—buffalo, maybe. Lions would be hard to see because their golden fur would be camouflaged by the grasses, so Callie listened carefully for a sound on the wind—the territorial roar of a male lion, or a mother lion calling for her baby.

"Let's be as quiet as we can," she whispered to her new friend. The lion cub meowed. "Shh, noisy one!"

Callie turned in circles, trying to distinguish the different sounds of the Serengeti. There was the swishing of the wind as it whipped across the grasses and occasional cries of birds. But there was no roar. Callie didn't know what to do next, but she had to do *something*.

"I have to find a way home," she said. "But not until we've found your mother."

A Suitable Name

"We're going to do some exploring," she said to the baby in her arms. The cub reached up its soft paw and patted her face. "I could cuddle you forever!" She laughed. "But we need to get you home. Look, there's a trail. We'll start by going that way."

Hoping the path through the grass was made by the footsteps of lions, Callie set off. After a short walk, she came to an area where the grasses had been crushed completely flat and in some places torn up. The earth beneath was brownish-yellow and scarred with deep scratches.

The cub whined. Callie put it down and let it sniff the ground.

"What is it, little lion? Is it a smell you know?"

While the cub turned in circles following its nose, Callie searched the ground for clues. Then she found one—a tuft of coarse orange hair. It must have come from a lion's mane! Had there been a fight—a clash between prides over food or territory?

In her mind, Callie pictured the battle, all claws and jaws and sharp, sharp teeth. Frightening sounds and little cubs running for safety across the vast Serengeti, searching for a place to hide. Callie hated to think her little cub might have been caught up in such a scary scene, but it looked like a possibility.

"Yes, this could be where you got lost," Callie said to the cub, who was still sniffing. "Come on. Your family isn't here now, but we will find them, I promise."

It was a big promise, and Callie hoped that she could keep it. It wasn't like the promises she normally made, such as playing with Emma at recess or scraping the plates after dinner. This was the Serengeti! She took a moment to look around. The landscape was empty and barren, and far, far away from anything she knew.

She raised her hand to shield her eyes from the light as she looked for lions or people or something that might help, but it was impossible to see. The heat was making the air ripple, the landscape bend, and the colors blend together. It was hard to focus on anything.

Meanwhile, the lion cub had started running away, almost tripping over its heavy paws.

Callie smiled. "You want to go that way, do you?"

But the cub wasn't following a trail or a scent. It was chasing a giant grasshopper. When Callie realized, she laughed so loudly that she took herself by surprise.

"That looks fun!" She joined in the chase, running alongside the cub in pursuit of the insect, getting close but never managing to catch it.

"This is impossible!" Callie panted. The cub was clearly thinking the same thing because it lay down with a big thump. Its chest was rising and falling fast, and Callie scooped up the cub in her arms.

"Weren't we silly, running around in the midday sun?" she said. She should have known better. The little lion was just a baby, and babies were vulnerable. Until they found the pride, Callie was its only chance of survival. If she really wanted to be a vet, now was the time to prove she had what it took.

"With hand on heart, I promise to care for animals in need of help, and I will not rest until they are well again. That's my very own vet's oath," Callie explained to the cub, who blinked back.

"That means I won't leave you until you're safe."

Under the shade of a tree, Callie laid the cub down and pulled off her backpack. There was a bottle of water inside it. She poured some of the water into her cupped hand, and the cub began to lap it up thirstily. Its tongue was prickly like sandpaper against her palm—the same as Emma's cat, Patches—and Callie shook her head in wonderment. Wasn't it incredible how house cats were so similar to these wild ones? The only difference really was size. Just think if Patches was the size of a lion…. They would need a bigger scratching post for starters, and he would bring home much larger things than mice. Looking at the cub now, it was hard to imagine that one day it would grow up to be a hunter. It looked more like a teddy bear!

When the cub finished drinking, Callie tried to swig the last bit of water from the bottle, but the cub brushed against her arm and knocked the bottle out of her hands. The rest of the water soaked into the ground. It didn't matter—at least the lion was looking brighter, although it was still a little wobbly on its legs. It needed food.

"Hang on," Callie said, remembering what was in her bag. "I have something you might like."

She had been much too excited to eat all of her lunch at the zoo. While the other kids sat at the tables scarfing their sandwiches and chips, Callie had been reading the posters pinned on the walls—

life cycles of insects, caring for baby animals, hostile environments, endangered species. In fact, she'd only nibbled half a sandwich and an apple before Mr. Vincent had begun telling them to "get a move on." She had been annoyed, but now it turned out that not finishing lunch was a blessing in disguise. She had leftover food for the cub.

Callie unwrapped her remaining sandwich. It was chicken and lettuce. She guessed lions didn't eat lettuce, but she held out the piece of cold roast chicken, and the cub took it between its teeth.

"I know you don't usually cook your meat, but it's all I've got, I'm afraid."

The cub gulped it down and then looked at her expectantly.

"More? I'm not sure if there is anything else…."

Callie rummaged in her lunch box. She didn't think an apple core would be welcome. Or her box of raisins.

"A-ha!" There, wrapped in foil, was something that might do. "I'm sure lions would eat eggs if there was nothing else on the menu. Maybe, if they were really, *really* hungry, they'd eat one that's hard-boiled."

The cub struggled with the texture at first but ate it all up, using its giant fluffy paw to brush away yellow yolk crumbs from its muzzle. Then it tried

to lick the crumbs that had stuck to
its paw, but that meant balancing
awkwardly on three legs. It wobbled,
fell, and rolled back onto its feet.

"You're a hilarious little cub!" Callie
exclaimed. She pulled the lion toward
her. "But I can't keep calling you 'cub'
or 'little lion.' You need a name."

The cub looked at her and replied
with a squeaky roar.

"I think it'll have to be one I can
pronounce!" she said. "You need a name
that is worldly and wise, because one
day I just know you're going to grow
up to be a magnificent…. Oh!" Callie
realized she had no idea if the cub was
a boy or girl. She took a quick look. "A
magnificent *lioness*!"

Callie placed the little lioness in the

grass next to her. It looked so at home here, so much part of the landscape. To give it a normal human name like Lily or Rosie just wouldn't do. A funny name like Patches wouldn't do, either. She needed a name that belonged in this world.

"How about Serengeti or Africa? No, those names are too big for a small cub…. Wait! We're in Tanzania, so how about Tanzy for short? It's pretty and sweet—now isn't that the perfect name for you?"

Tanzy batted her paw clumsily at a fly that kept buzzing around her nose. Callie let her play while she concentrated on what to do next. Thinking hard, she remembered that north of the Serengeti was the Mara

River. It was where some of the great migrations took place. Animals crossed over it to look for cooler temperatures and more food in the Masai Mara Park on the other side, in the nearby country of Kenya. The Mara River was a source of water and food. In fact, it could be just the place to find a pride of lions, tired and thirsty from a fight.

"That's it, Tanzy!" Callie exclaimed. "We need to find the river!"

The Sound of Thunder

Callie was finding it hard to pack away her lunch box with Tanzy leaping all over her. The little cub was gaining more and more confidence every minute! She wriggled and climbed, and Callie had to pick her up and put her back down on the ground.

"I love you, too!" She sighed happily. "But let me organize my bag. We can't leave any litter behind."

But then Tanzy wrapped her front

paws around Callie's arm, weighing it
down, and started to nibble on Callie's
thumb.

"Ow! Those little teeth of yours are
sharp!"

With her free hand, Callie grabbed
Tanzy's muzzle lightly and Tanzy clawed
back, trying to get her teeth into Callie's
wrist. It didn't hurt; it just tickled.

"You're suddenly very playful, so I guess you must be feeling better."

Without warning, Tanzy leaped onto her shoulder, and the two of them rolled in the grass. Tanzy was getting more excited by the rough-and-tumble action, and Callie was loving every moment. This could be the only chance she ever got to be a lion cub's playmate.

But play-fighting wasn't something cubs did just for fun—it helped to train them in the skills of hunting and killing. Being away from the pride meant Tanzy could be missing out on important life lessons from her siblings and parents. And if Tanzy didn't learn to be the hunter, then she could end up being the prey. Without her lion skills, she'd never survive the Serengeti.

The truth made Callie focus. She had
to deliver the cub to safety and then find
a way home. She had no more water, and
her throat was starting to scratch with
thirst. There was no time to lose. Callie
grabbed Tanzy gently by the scruff of
her neck, just as a mother lion would do,
and put her down on the ground.

"Enough horsing around. We have a
river to find."

Heaving the bag over her shoulder,
Callie stepped out of the shade of the
tree and immediately felt the heat tingle
on her skin. Tanzy trotted to her side,
ready for the next step in their adventure.

"That's right, Tanzy. I want you
to stay by my side every step of the
way," Callie said, smiling down at her
companion. "Just as soon as I figure

out which way to go...."

With no idea where in the Serengeti she was, how would ever find the Mara River?

A group of birds flew overhead—seven or eight of them, all in a straight line. They were brown and white, with huge, finger-tipped wings, skinny necks, and long, thin legs. *They look like herons or cranes*, Callie thought. *They could be water birds!*

Tanzy had spotted another huge grasshopper and was about to bound away on a hopeless mission to catch it.

"Oh, no, you don't…," Callie scolded. She steered the cub away gently with her foot. "There's no time to chase grasshoppers. We have to follow the birds!"

Striding through the grasses under the blazing sun, Callie became uncomfortably hot. Her clothes were sticky, and her feet were baking in her shoes. If this had been a family walk or a PE lesson, she would have sat on the ground and refused to move another inch. But she had a promise to keep, and that kept her going.

"It … can't … be … far … now," she puffed. "Look, Tanzy. More water birds, and they're flying in the same direction as the first flock. We have to be close!"

Tanzy seemed to understand the encouragement in her voice and meowed.

Heat rippled the air, and except for the chirrup of locusts and grasshoppers, the plains were eerily quiet. There was nothing but the noise of their footsteps scuffing the ground and the occasional whoosh of the breeze through the grasses. Tanzy bounced ahead and Callie walked steadily on behind, one foot after the other, eyes on the sky to see which way the birds were flying.

A drumming sound interrupted her rhythm.

What was that? It reminded her of horses, like hooves pummeling dry earth. Callie searched the horizon for a clue, but there was nothing out there, and it was getting louder. Within seconds, the hoof beats were rumbling like incoming thunder, and the vibrations coursed through Callie's body.

She spun around and there behind her, in a flurry of brown dust, was a stampeding herd. The charging beasts were large and gray. They were approaching so fast that it wasn't long before she could see their bony backs, grizzly beards, and sharp horns.

"Wildebeest!" she exclaimed. "Tanzy!"

Callie scooped Tanzy off the ground. Clutching the cub tight to her chest, she ran to the closest tree. The acacia tree with its umbrella canopy had plenty of branches to climb, if there was time....

The wildebeest were so close now that she could see the flare of their nostrils and the way they lowered their horned heads as if they were butting the air in front of them!

"Quick, Tanzy!" She raised the cub as high up the trunk as she could reach. "Climb!"

The cub scrambled to the top, but Callie knew there'd be no time to follow safely. If she slipped and fell, she'd be trampled. She flattened herself against the trunk, arms tight against her body. The animals stampeded by, streaming by either side of the tree, which was now like an island in a fast-flowing river of wildebeest. The noise was deafening. The hooves sent the dusty earth billowing up in clouds. Callie closed her eyes tightly.

When it was over, she sighed with relief. "Who knew herbivores could be so dangerous!"

Callie wiped the dust from her eyes and looked up. The cub was high up in the tree, shaking.

"It's okay—you can come down now."

But Tanzy looked paralyzed with fear.

"Hang on, little one!" Callie began
to climb the cat's cradle of branches,
pulling herself to the top where the cub
was shivering. She reached out, and
Tanzy leaped right into her arms and
hid her face in Callie's neck.

Comforting the cub, Callie stopped
to catch her breath and take a look at
the view. The tree wasn't very tall,
but being higher up allowed her to see
right across the land. As the disturbed
earth settled, Callie noticed something
ahead—a huge glittering ribbon, looping
and snaking through the landscape. No
more than a mile or two away.

"The Mara River!"

Journey to the Mara

Callie stayed a little while longer in the
tree, sitting in the fork of two branches,
swinging her legs. As the warm wind
fluttered her hair, she began to laugh.
Only moments before she had been
tired and frightened, but now she felt
more alive than ever. Was it the dry
Serengeti air? The view of the great
Mara River in the distance? Maybe
it was the thrill of the stampeding
wildebeest....

"Why do you think I feel this way, huh?" she asked the cub. Tanzy gave her neck a prickly lick. "Oh, you think it's because of you, do you? You know, Tanzy, I thought I'd go home today without seeing any lions at all. Now look at me, right here in the land of the lions. And I've got a feeling it was you who brought me here."

Was it dust in the cub's eye, or did Tanzy actually wink?

"Come on. It's probably time we both went home."

Callie carefully climbed back down the tree with Tanzy in one arm. After the race of the wildebeest, the plains were calm once again. Callie marveled at how everything could be so dramatic one minute and sleepy and serene the next. The sun-bathed landscape was almost hypnotic.

Heat played a lot of tricks—it made everything on the horizon look like liquid. She had once read a story about a desert mirage, where the heat took away all the color of the sand so it looked like water. In the story, the thirsty travelers thought it was an oasis in the distance.

Was that what she was seeing now, over there?

Just up ahead—too close to be the river—the ground was fuzzy and out of focus. It was shimmering. What *was* that? She hadn't seen it from her position in the tree. It looked like a silvery sheet. It looked like water. *Water....* Callie felt her throat tighten. There were waterholes in the Serengeti—maybe one would be fed by a freshwater spring. She licked her dry lips at the thought of cool, clean water and began to run toward it.

But the closer she got, the more confused she became. There was still a shimmer, but in it she noticed a nose and two ears. Four tails. Then individual shapes began to emerge from the confusing pattern. Callie could see now.

The animals' stripes meant that from
a distance, they had no solid outline—
they melted together into one large
mass. It was impossible to tell what
they were.

"Oh my goodness!" Callie gasped.
"That is the most clever camouflage
I've ever seen!"

The dazzle of zebras parted as
Callie walked right through them,
eyes wide in
amazement.

They looked like stubby striped horses—something that could have been conjured up by a wizard. Even their manes were striped! Callie wished Emma could see this—she was the world's biggest lover of zebras. Callie felt a lump in her throat at the thought of her friend, who would be missing her. But all she had to do to feel better was look at Tanzy and remember her vet's oath.

Callie and Tanzy continued on toward the Mara River. The closer they got, the more animals they saw emerging from the plains. They walked alongside graceful gazelles and impalas with twisty horns and pretty patterns. Callie's stomach fluttered with excitement— she was so close to Africa's incredible wildlife! It also fluttered with fear, because among the Serengeti's native animals were some very dangerous species. If other animals were coming to the river, then the dangerous ones would be coming, too.

Keeping an eye out for sudden stampedes, Callie kept going. The sun beating down on her head made her sleepy. Her dry eyes blinked against the hot air and dust. But just a few more minutes and they'd be there. Then they would find the pride, and she could concentrate on getting home.

The Mara River wasn't as Callie had imagined. The pictures at the zoo had shown raging torrents and animals struggling to get through the fast waters, but over the summer, there hadn't been much rain in the Serengeti, and the river was low. Large rocks created stepping stones across it, and areas of the riverbed stuck out of the shallow waters, making sandy islands for birds and tired beasts to sit on. Callie had no idea that so many different animals—some of which she was sure would like to eat each other—could rest happily side by side.

"Should we take a closer look, Tanzy? Do you think they'll make room for us?"

There were antelope, wildebeest, and zebras drinking. Hippos basked on rocks or bobbed around in small pools, some with birds standing on their heads. Callie looked left and right. There were birds and beasts as far as the eye could see. But where were the lions?

Callie turned in circles, hoping to see a glimpse of golden fur among the brown and gray, but there was no sign of them.

"Oh, Tanzy, they're not here," Callie

said. She tried to stay calm in case the
cub got upset. But her heart was racing.
She was so certain they'd be here. They
might have crossed the waters, Callie
supposed, although on the other side
she could see … elephants! Wow!

The peaceful herd of beautiful creatures stood at the water's edge, their trunks swaying and their ears flapping gently. They were happy.

And then, suddenly, they weren't.

Without warning, a large elephant broke into a run. It headed away from the river and into the foliage behind. Its ear-splitting trumpet blasted the air like a danger siren, and then the other members of its herd began running, too. They were fast on their feet, trampling the bushes and small trees to get away.

Then other animals at the edge of the river began to panic. Impalas backed away from the water, stepping on top of one another as they fled. Callie's heart started beating so fast that she could feel it against her ribs. She couldn't see anything, but she sensed trouble. The air seemed to fizz with electricity. Tanzy picked up on it, too. Her eyes were wide and scared.

"What's going on, Tanzy?"

Callie searched for a sign, but it didn't look as if there had been a crocodile attack or any hippos getting feisty. In fact, all the animals in the river were calm. It was the animals on land that were shrieking and bucking and jumping in all directions. The commotion got louder and louder.

Tanzy knew what was happening, though. The cub was looking to the right, roaring over and over at an invisible enemy. Callie followed her line of sight.

Cheetahs.

Danger, Everywhere!

Callie and Tanzy stood absolutely still.
Farther around the bend of the river—
less than a soccer pitch away—three
cheetahs were making their way through
a clump of trees. They walked slowly
and carefully, spread out in a line. Callie
guessed it was how they attacked—from
all angles.

With every step they took, a wave
of animals scattered, and soon there
were beasts running everywhere, herds

colliding in panic. If Callie and Tanzy didn't move now, they'd either be trampled or on a cheetah's menu!

"Let's go!" Callie grabbed Tanzy, who was still roaring bravely, and pulled her up into her arms. Which way should they go? With wildebeest, deer, zebras, and cheetahs running wild, there was nowhere safe. She spotted a stack of rocks to her left, a few feet back from the river. Cheetahs would be able to climb them easily, but they had their sights set on the water, where a group of young gazelles was caught in the muddy shallows. Callie scrambled up one of the rocks, clutching Tanzy tightly. The cub's paws and head rested over one of Callie's shoulders as she continued to roar at the cheetahs.

"Don't be scared," Callie said,
although at that moment she was as
scared as she'd ever been. She turned
to look at the scene by the river.

The cheetahs were still heading
for the water, closing in like a net—
walking slowly, occasionally lying low,

getting closer and closer. And then—
the sprint! The cheetahs burst into
a run so fast it took Callie's breath
away. The gazelles, croaking and
bleating in panic, struggled in the
mud. Most of them broke free and
scampered away, zigzagging across the
land to confuse the cats, but one was
stuck, its thin legs wedged into the
riverbed.

Callie hoped it would get away in
time, but if it did, then the cheetahs
would go hungry. *This is nature*, she
reminded herself. *Beautiful but cruel.*
She turned away. She didn't want to see
what would happen next. She buried
her face in Tanzy's fur and kept it there
until Tanzy, no longer roaring, gave her
a nudge under her chin.

Callie looked
up. The little
gazelle was
covered in
mud but
bounding
away across
the plains while the
cheetahs slunk back into
the trees.

"That was one lucky gazelle," she said.
Tanzy gave her a big prickly lick right
across her cheek. "Now it's time we made
sure you have a happy ending, too!"

But she didn't have a clue what to do or
where to go. She'd been so sure the lions
would be at the river that she hadn't
planned what to do if they weren't there.

She looked out over the plains. The

Serengeti was so big and wild. She and Tanzy were just two small animals, and suddenly, Callie didn't feel so brave about her mission. On top of that, she had started to feel shaky. Her stomach groaned with hunger, and her throat was raw and dry. Her head was dizzy with heat. She sat down quickly before her legs gave way.

She looked at Tanzy in her lap. The cub's eyes were half closed.

"Do you need a nap, little one?" Callie said, gently rubbing Tanzy's head. "Or are you feeling weak, like me?"

Tanzy tried to roar, but nothing came out—not even a squeak—and Callie felt hot tears in her eyes. This cub needed food and her mother's milk soon, or she might not survive. Mr. Tom's words echoed in her mind. *Being a vet is a tough job … but it looks to me like you have determination….*

If Mr. Tom could see her now, maybe he wouldn't think she had what it took. But being a vet was all she wanted to do, so she had to find strength and determination from somewhere.

"I made a vet's oath, and I can't break it," she said aloud.

Callie closed her eyes, breathed in deeply, and gathered her thoughts. Before she decided where to go next, Tanzy needed attention.

"Lions get most of their moisture from food. But you've only had some dry chicken and a tiny egg. That's where we'll start—we'll get you a drink of water."

Cradling Tanzy, Callie headed away

from the remaining wildebeest and along the riverbank. When she found an area where there were no animals that could run, jump, or cause a commotion, she approached the water's edge. Tanzy started to wriggle in her arms, as if she could smell the water.

"Wait, Tanzy," Callie said. "I'm not going to put you down yet. Not until I'm absolutely sure it's safe. I've read about crocodiles, and I don't think I'd like to meet one!"

Callie threw a few big sticks into the shallows in front of her. If there was a crocodile there, it would leap or wriggle with surprise—or attack. But after each splash, the water was still.

Holding on tight to Tanzy's body, she let the cub lap.

The sun-sparkles danced on the
river, and Callie was tempted to dip
her hand into it and cup some of the
water to her mouth. But this wasn't a
freshwater spring, and Callie knew that
her stomach would not be used to the
bacteria in the water. It could make her
sick. And what use was a sick vet?

She pushed her thirst from her mind and instead concentrated on staying alert and being ready to run, just like an animal of the Serengeti.

After drinking, Tanzy broke away from her grip and tried to hop across some rocks by the bank to investigate the birds perched there.

"No you don't, little one." Callie was so parched her voice was just a whisper now. "There'll be plenty of time to play when you find your brothers and sisters."

But where were Tanzy's siblings? Where were her mother and father? Where would she and Tanzy even start to look for them?

She took out the postcard—it was the only clue she had.

Serengeti Daze

The lioness in the picture was now
sitting on her hind legs, her head high.
Other lionesses were standing next
to her, peering in different directions.
They were on the lookout.

"Where are you?" Callie whispered,
running her finger across the picture. She
felt her fingertips tingle. Then she
recognized a patch of flattened grass
behind the pride, a little way in the
distance.

"Tanzy, they're waiting for you," Callie said, brightening. "They haven't given up and moved on at all. Of course! If it was me, I'd be staying close to where I lost you…. So that's where we should go—back to where it all started." That place with the claw marks and tufts of lion mane—that was where the cub had gotten lost. The pride would have found a safe place to rest or hide, but they wouldn't have moved too far away from where the cub went missing.

"No one could abandon you, Tanzy," Callie said to the now lively cub.

Callie looked again at the Mara River and the lush green fields and trees on the other side of it. It felt wrong to be walking away from it, but she was certain it was the right thing to do.

She turned around, and with Tanzy at her side, began walking against the tide of deer heading for the river. The deer leaped aside when they got near but then regrouped and continued their journey. In this heat, any sensible animal would be heading for water. Once again, Callie had to push away thoughts of fresh water and how freely it flowed back home.

Home. She suddenly missed it like crazy. She missed the cool air. She missed crisp apples and fruit juice and sliced-up cucumbers. She missed her soft bed. Any bed. She was so tired that she could sleep anywhere—up an acacia tree, in the long grasses, on a Serengeti rock…. She just needed sleep.

Tanzy brushed against her ankle and gave a little squeak, looking up at her and blinking against the bright sunlight. Callie jolted awake. She'd been walking with her eyes closed in a daze! She woke herself up by shaking out her arms and legs.

"I'm going to be strong for you, Tanzy," Callie said, holding back the tears. "I made a promise as a vet and as your friend."

Callie knew that she would never break her promise. She just hoped that the wild Serengeti wouldn't break her first.

Callie tripped and stumbled across the land. She kept her eyes on Tanzy as she repeated her vet's oath, over and over. It kept her going when she thought she might melt in the heat. But although she forced her brain to stay focused, Callie's legs were tiring. Her footsteps slowed down until eventually she came to a stop.

She couldn't take another step. Tanzy circled her and pawed at her legs with worry.

"I'm okay, Tanzy, I'm okay," Callie whispered, sitting down. "But we've been walking a very long time. Give me a minute to rest, and we'll be on our way again."

Even as she was saying the words, Callie felt her body sinking lower into the grass. She fell asleep before her head even touched the ground.

Callie felt a tickling on her cheek. What was that? In her sleepy daze, she thought it was Tanzy's whiskers and smiled, but as the tickling spread across her face and down her neck, she woke in alarm.

Ants! Ugh! Callie leaped up, brushing the little brown ants from her face and neck. Even after she'd gotten rid of them, she kept wriggling and itching as if they were still crawling on her. What a horrible feeling! Her head wasn't any better, either—it hurt from sleeping out in the sun. But that wasn't the worst thing.

Tanzy was nowhere to be seen.

Callie looked out across the plains. The

sun was low, and the blue sky had turned pink-orange, like a ripe apricot. How long had she been asleep? How long had the cub been missing?

"Tanzy!" she called. Her thirsty voice was so cracked that it didn't carry far. "Tanzy, where are you?"

Callie sat back down and held her head in her hands. Everything hurt. Her head ached, and her heart was sore…. Tanzy … little Tanzy….

She couldn't give up. If she did, she'd be no good to anyone. Callie squeezed her eyes shut and took several deep breaths to calm herself down.

Another annoying ant found its way onto her face, and she brushed it away with the back of her hand. It came back again, this time with friends. She felt their footsteps tickle her chin. She wanted to scream. She opened her eyes, ready to leap up and pat herself down....

Oh! Tanzy nuzzled her chin. It wasn't ants—it *was* whiskers this time!

"Thank goodness!" Callie said. She still felt like crying but this time with relief. The cub was safe. "Come for a hug. I could really use one."

But Tanzy had different ideas. She ran ahead into the grasses, then stopped and looked back. Then she did the same thing again and again.

"Do you want me to follow you?"

Callie rose to her feet, wobbling like a tree in a heat haze. She didn't feel like she had the energy to start walking again just yet, but the lions might be close. Concentrating on putting one foot in front of the other, she followed Tanzy. Callie didn't notice the strange-looking creature ahead of them until.... *Snoo-ink!* The noise was like a long pig's oink. But it wasn't a pig.

The weird animal looked like an enormous ferret with a stripe of gray fur on top and black fur underneath, and it was leaning over a large broken tree branch. Callie narrowed her eyes and tried to focus. As she stepped closer, it turned and bared its teeth before running away.

"What was that, Tanzy?" Callie said. But the cub knew exactly what it was. She had already run to where the creature had been and was licking at the branch, where a couple of sleepy bees were circling. Dark amber liquid oozed from a hole in the top.

So hungry her tummy was twisting in knots, Callie decided that if it was good enough for a lion, it was good enough for her.... She scooped some of the sticky liquid onto her finger and tasted it. Such sweetness! Callie's face lit up.

"Wonderful raw honey! That must have been a honey badger. I remember seeing it in my animal encyclopedia. We're lucky, Tanzy. Honey badgers can be vicious. Did you see those teeth?"

Tanzy wasn't listening. She was

feasting, making funny, snarly faces
as she tried to lick the honey sticking
to her gums. Callie scooped out more
honey for herself. She licked her finger
with a satisfying slurp. She might have
missed out on ice cream back at the zoo,
but this was the sweetest thing she'd
ever tasted.

"Clever bees for making the honey. Clever badger for finding the hive. And clever Tanzy for sniffing it out. You're the best!"

The natural sugars in the honey filled her with energy. She felt amazing. This was power food, and it was delicious. Tanzy thought so, too, although the cub was now struggling with her sticky whiskers and was trying to reach her tongue all around her face.

"Come on, funny thing!" Callie laughed. "Let's leave some honey for the poor badger. I've got a feeling he was too weak to fight and needs that honey to build his strength. Besides, it's time we got you some proper lion food!"

A Familiar Sound

Her throat was still dry, but the honey had given her energy. There would be no more sleeping now. Not until Tanzy was safely home. Callie felt determined. Now there was nothing but a stretch of grassland between them and the pride. She and Tanzy set off once again, this time with a skip and a made-up song.

Full of love and honey inside, we'll keep going until we find Tanzy's pride!

In Callie's rush of happiness, she

forgot about the dangers around them.
Then a sudden screech stopped her in
her tracks. A chill went down her spine.
She didn't know what it was, but it could
only be an animal of some sort, and
there was nowhere to hide. She tucked
Tanzy under her arm and crouched
in the long grasses. She gathered her
Serengeti wits and listened closely.

There it was again…. The horrible
noise was made up of ten, maybe
twenty different voices. Peeking over the
grass, she saw a group of fluffy, spotted
animals running at full speed. Hyenas!
Everyone knew about hyenas. They were
pack hunters, and they were known to
attack humans.

The hyenas were running as fast as
their legs could carry them, but Callie

couldn't see what they were chasing. There was nothing in front of them.

Eventually they slowed and stopped. Some sat on the ground exhausted, and others paced around them. Their screeches turned to laughter. The cackling sound made Callie want to giggle. But they weren't laughing—they were bickering among themselves. Callie turned away. She didn't want to see any more fights, and besides, she was busy trying to figure something out.

If those hyenas hadn't been chasing something, then maybe they were running *from* something ... and there was only one beast that scared hyenas that much.

Lions!

Scanning the land, Callie couldn't see any, but that didn't mean they weren't there. Her heart began to pound— she was excited for Tanzy but also frightened. In her short experience in the Serengeti, she knew animals could appear out of nowhere—running across the plains, hunting or being hunted.... She suddenly felt very exposed. Standing in the middle of the plains with no speed in her legs and a small cub to care for meant she was as vulnerable as a gazelle and not even half as fast. Callie thought of all the animals she'd seen that day. If you're not tough like a wildebeest, if you can't run fast like a deer, if you can't attack like a cheetah … what do you do? Then Callie remembered the zebras. Camouflage!

She grabbed handfuls of the golden grasses and stuffed them into her clothing and hair. She now looked like a scarecrow, and she itched like crazy all over, but if she stayed low, she'd be well hidden.

There was an outcrop in the distance close to the fighting spot. She could rest and think about her next move there. If she hadn't had all that honey, she would never have made it, and Callie thanked Tanzy once more with a good scratch behind the ears. Then they were on their way, running low and fast through the grasses toward the outcrop.

At the base of it, they sat down in the shade of a tree and caught their breath. Grasshoppers popped out of the grasses all around them, but Tanzy didn't seem interested. She looked at Callie and let out a squeaky roar.

"Are you trying to tell me something?" Callie said, reaching for her. But Tanzy backed away and roared again. Callie jumped to her feet. "What is it, Tanzy?"

Then she heard it for herself. A low grumble that echoed against the giant stones. Tanzy went perfectly still. Callie gasped.

"It's your pride. They're calling for you."

Callie bubbled with excitement. This was what they'd been waiting for. She wanted to gather Tanzy in her arms and deliver her to the lioness and say, "I took care of her for you," but she knew that wouldn't be possible.

"Your mother desperately wants to see you, Tanzy," she said, crouching down to look into the cub's eyes. "But I don't think she'll want to see me. She might think I took you away from her."

Tanzy snapped at a passing fly, revealing her tiny, razor-sharp teeth.

"Or she might be hungry," Callie added with a gulp.

The lioness's call came again. Tanzy walked a few paces ahead before turning back to look at Callie.

"Yes, Tanzy, it's time to go," Callie said, putting on a brave smile. Tanzy stared at her and didn't move. "Come on, then, I'll walk some of the way with you."

Together they walked around the base of the outcrop. The lions must have sensed Tanzy was near because their roars weren't low and long and sad— they burst high and loud and full of hope. Callie was frightened now. This wasn't Pride of Place. There was no fence between her and Africa's most famous killer cats. It would be silly to go any farther.

She crouched down, took Tanzy's face in her hands, and looked into those sweet brown eyes for the final time.

"You'll have to do the last part on your own."

Tanzy leaped into her arms.

"Oh! I am going to miss you, too," Callie sniffed. "But this is how it has to be. This is your world, not mine."

Tanzy pressed her soft triangle nose against Callie's cheek. Then Callie let go and gave her a nudge.

"Go," she whispered. "I promised to take care of you, and I did. Now I promise never to forget you, and I won't. I could never forget you, Tanzy."

A Bittersweet Reunion

Callie began to climb the rocks as fast
as she could. She didn't stop until
she reached the top, where she found
a scrubby bush to hide behind. She
looked down at the grassland below
where Tanzy was moving unsteadily
toward the sound of her mother's
voice. Callie ran to the other side of
the outcrop's large, flat top to look
down. She gasped. The entire pride was
there—two lions, five lionesses, and

seven little cubs. They were sitting in the shade. All but one.

The lioness had started running. Even from way up in the air, Callie could tell by the bounce in her legs that she was a very happy mother. She stopped and roared again—a deep, thick, reverberating sound. Very soon, she would be reunited with her cub.

Callie wanted to cheer, whoop, and clap, but she had to be silent. She was in the presence of powerful animals. She clamped her hand over her mouth to stop her excited squeals from escaping.

Then there was a roar like she'd never heard before. It was roar of triumph and an announcement—the cub has returned!

All the lions got to their feet as the lost lion came into view. Then—the joy! Tanzy's mother circled her, sniffing and nuzzling. They rubbed cheeks. They roared in short, happy bursts. The other lionesses began running, too, their long tails dancing behind them. Soon Tanzy was engulfed in the love and relief of her mother and aunts, and her brothers and sisters were now springing toward the huddle as fast as their little legs could carry them.

When Tanzy emerged from between the legs of the adult lions, the cubs rolled together on the ground in one big, fluffy bundle. The largest male lion roared. Then they got up and shook the Serengeti dust from their coats. It was time to move on. The two males led the way, and the females ushered the playful cubs, making sure every member of the pride was there.

Callie felt her heart thump as the pride started to move away from their resting place, padding deeper into the

color-changing scenery of the Serengeti.
The yellow sun had melted into a soft
orange and hung low in the sky, turning
the grasses a rosy gold. The acacia and
baobab trees turned to dark silhouettes
with long shadows.

Callie watched as the lions' shadows
followed in a row behind them. The
smallest one at the back belonged to
Tanzy, who now looked tiny in the
distance.

"Bye-bye, Tanzy," Callie whispered,
her eyes welling with tears. The cub
suddenly stopped and looked back up at
her. Callie waved and laughed.

But the lioness wasn't going to lose her
cub again—she gave her a hefty bat in the
right direction with her paw, and Tanzy
skidded ahead.

Callie stayed on the rock a while
longer, enjoying the cooling breeze and
watching the sun go down. It oozed like
lava and sizzled on the horizon, and the
first star of the night sat high in the
peach-and-purple sky like a diamond.
With Tanzy safe, Callie had time to
appreciate the magic and beauty of the
Serengeti. It was wide and wild. It was
totally wonderful.

But it wasn't home.

She pulled out her postcard. The
light was fading, but the pictures were
still clear. The image of the pride had
changed. It wasn't lying down but
walking, a group of lions, big and small,
all facing the same direction. Callie held
her breath and crossed her fingers. It
was time to check up on her little lost

cub. Was her job done? Could she go home? She tilted the card.

A lion cub stood on its own, its pride in the distance. Its head was cocked to one side, and its eyes danced with curiosity. It looked strong and full of health.

"Go, Tanzy!" Callie laughed. "Hurry and don't stop to play with any grasshoppers on the way!"

She closed her eyes and kissed the picture of her rescued little lion as the cooling breeze brushed across her face.

A Special Gift

"Callie! Come on!"

What? Callie's eyes sprang open. She turned in circles. No dust, no heat, no sunset. She was back!

"When did it g-g-get so cold?" she stammered, her teeth chattering as she joined Emma, who was waiting farther along the walkway.

"It's not cold. And what's this?" Emma began to pick strands of grass from Callie's hair. "Are you turning into a farmer?"

"I don't know," Callie said. "I—what—what's going on?"

Emma shook her head. "Oh, no!"

Mr. Tom appeared. "What's the matter here?"

"Callie has been brainwashed. I think it's those monkeys over there. They look mean."

Mr. Tom laughed. "Enough monkey business—I promised I'd have you back in ten minutes."

Emma wagged her finger at the monkeys. "You leave my friend alone."

While Emma was scolding the monkeys, Callie tried to pull herself together. She had walked for hours in the Serengeti, but not a minute had passed back home. Even so, her skin had grown used to the African sun, and now she was freezing. She rubbed her arms to get warm.

"Cold?" Mr. Tom asked. "Imagine how the lions feel—living here in a cold climate when they should be in the Serengeti."

"Hmmm," Callie said, nodding. Although she didn't have to imagine.

Back at the gift shop, Mrs. Mullins, Mr. Vincent, and the assistant teachers had lined the children up in a row, ready to board the bus.

"There they are!" shouted a girl named Samira.

"We thought you'd been eaten by a lion," said Milos.

Sarah shook her head. "I bet they didn't see any lions at all."

Emma nudged Callie and gave her a big wink. "We did, actually," she said confidently. "We saw a ton of lions. They were great, weren't they, Callie?"

"Yep," Callie nodded.

"Really?" Sarah's jaw dropped open.

"How many male lions were there again, Callie?"

"Two."

"That's right. Two. And there were three lionesses."

"Five," Callie corrected.

"Oh yeah, five. And a bunch of cubs."

"Eight in total," Callie said, and she couldn't stop a wide smile from spreading across her face.

As they left the shop, she grabbed some of the free flyers, including *African Animals*, which came with a map of the

Serengeti on the back.

When she was seated on the bus, she began to mark on the page where she had been. She drew in acacia trees and stampeding herds, zebra dazzles, attacking cheetahs, and loping giraffes. Next she filled the blue band of the Mara River with hippo heads and penned a honey badger and some hyenas. Then she carefully sketched a pride of lions next to a stack of rocks. Looking down on them from the top, she drew herself.

"What's that—a monkey?"

Emma had grown bored of playing plastic-spider pranks, and Dan had pinched her cuddly snake.

"No, that's me."

"You? You wouldn't survive a day in

the Spaghetti."

"Do you mean Serengeti?" Callie said.

Emma started shrieking with laughter, and Callie laughed along with her. She was the funniest person in the world.

"It's a shame that you didn't get a real gift," Emma said, pointing at Callie's postcard.

Callie smiled. *But I did. I got to rescue a very special lion,* she said to herself as she tilted the card.

And Tanzy, head to one side, winked back.

ABOUT THE AUTHOR

Rachel Delahaye was born in Australia but has lived in the UK since she was six years old. She studied linguistics and worked as a magazine writer and editor before becoming a children's author. She loves words and animals; when she can combine the two, she is very happy indeed! At home, Rachel loves to read, write, and watch wildlife documentaries. She loves to go walking in the woods. She also follows news about animal rights and the environment and hopes that one day the world will be a better home for all species, not just humans!

Rachel lives in the beautiful city of Bath, England, with her two lively children and a dog named Rocket.